THIS BLOOMSBURY BOOK

BELONGS TO

....

TOO PICKLY!

JEAN REIDY

ILLUSTRATED BY GENEVIÈVE LELOUP

BLOOMSBURY

LONDON BERLIN NEW YORK

TOO FRUITY,

TOO FISHY!

TOO SLIMY,

TOO SLURPY,

TOO...

My favourite food is:

.... (yummy)

.... (scrummy)

.... (in my tummy!)

My favourite drink is:

.... (cold)

.... (hot)

.... (like it a lot!)

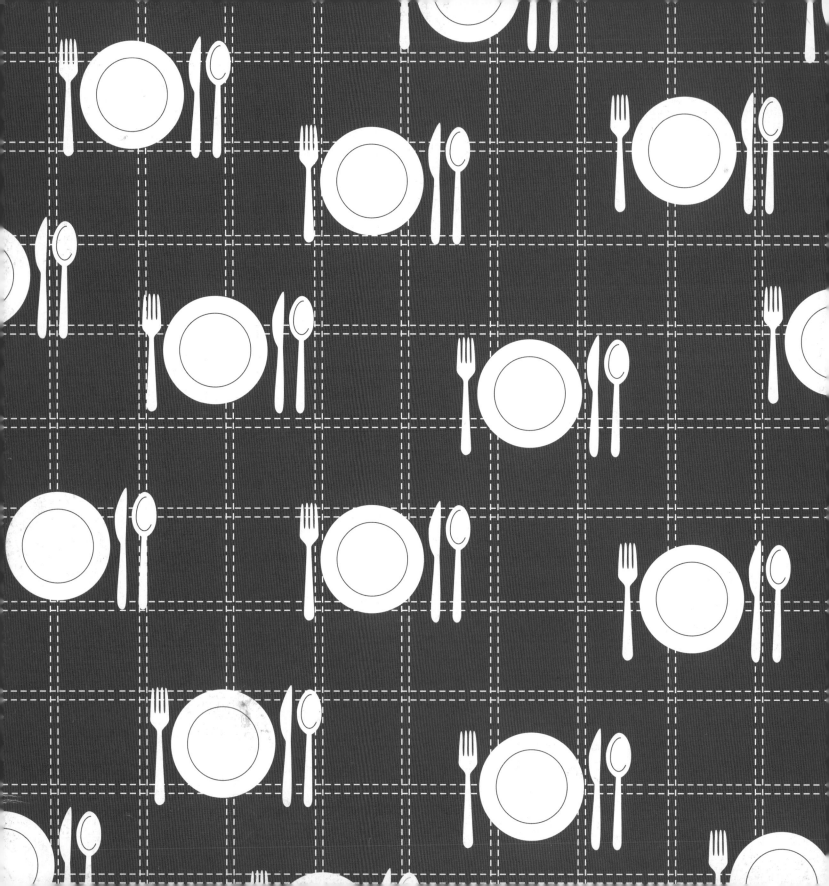

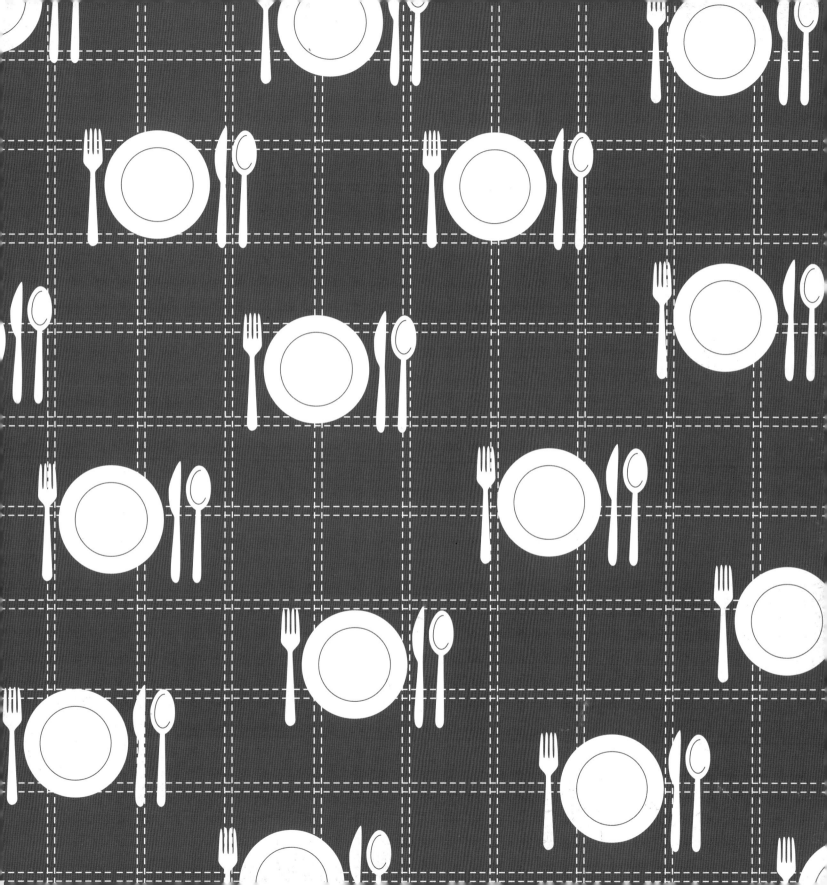

To Frank,
who loved his hot dogs —
peeled, please
J. R.

To little foodie Miss V
G. L.

Bloomsbury Publishing, London, Berlin and New York

First published in Great Britain in July 2010 by Bloomsbury Publishing Plc
36 Soho Square, London, W1D 3QY

First published in the USA in 2010 by Bloomsbury USA
175 Fifth Avenue, New York, NY 10010

Text copyright © Jean Reidy 2010
Illustrations copyright © Geneviève Leloup 2010
The moral rights of the author and illustrator have been asserted

A CIP catalogue record of this book is available from the British Library

ISBN 978 1 4088 0711 8

Printed in China by Hung Hing Printing Co. Ltd, Shenzhen, Guangdong

1 3 5 7 9 10 8 6 4 2

All papers used by Bloomsbury Publishing are natural, recyclable products made from
wood grown in well-managed forests. The manufacturing processes conform to the
environmental regulations of the country of origin

www.bloomsbury.com/childrens